GOLDILOCKS
AND
THE THREE BEARS

Retold by Janet Hillman   Illustrated by Pat Reynolds

Once upon a time
there were three bears.

There was a
great big
Papa Bear.

There was a
middle-sized
Mama Bear.

And there was a
teeny-weeny Baby Bear.

They all lived together
in a house in the woods.

They had three chairs —
a **great big** chair
for Papa Bear,

a **middle-sized** chair
for Mama Bear,

and a **teeny-weeny** chair
for Baby Bear.

They had three beds —
a **great big** bed
for Papa Bear,

a **middle-sized** bed
for Mama Bear,

and a teeny-weeny bed
for Baby Bear.

And they had three bowls
for their porridge.

One morning the porridge was too hot.

So the three bears went for a walk in the woods while it cooled.

Someone else was walking
in the woods that morning.

It was a little girl
with golden hair.
Her name was Goldilocks.

She saw the three bears' house.
"I wonder who lives here,"
she said.
And she walked inside.

Goldilocks saw the three
bowls of porridge.

She tasted the porridge in
the **great big** bowl.
But it was much too hot.

She tasted the porridge in
the **middle-sized** bowl.
But it was too hot, too.

She tasted the porridge in
the **teeny-weeny** bowl.
And it was just right.
So she ate it all up.

Goldilocks saw the three chairs.

She sat in

the **great big** chair.

But it was too high.

She sat in
the **middle-sized** chair
But it was too wide.

She sat in
the **teeny-weeny** chair.
And it was just right . . .
but then it broke.

Goldilocks saw the three beds.
She lay down on
the **great big** bed.
But it was too hard.

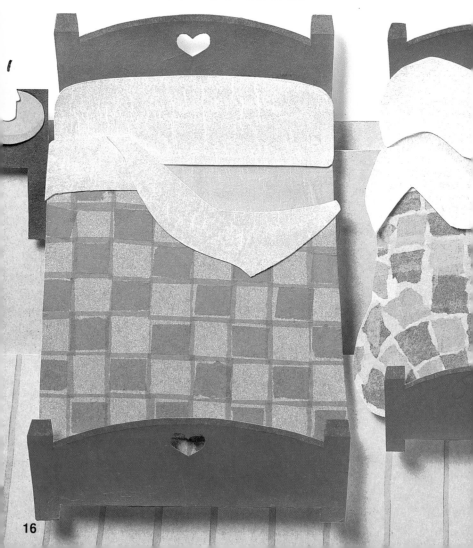

She lay down on
the **middle-sized** bed.
But it was too soft.

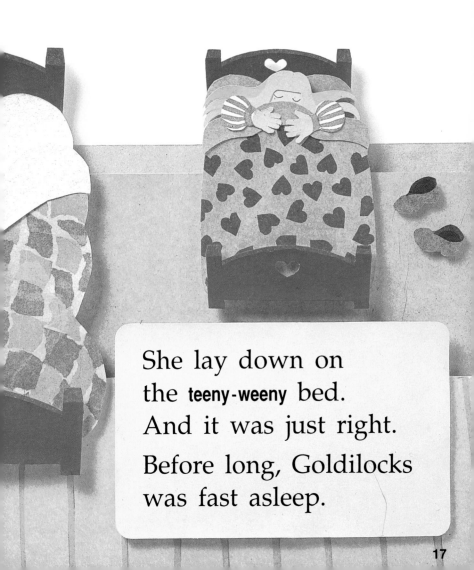

She lay down on
the teeny-weeny bed.
And it was just right.

Before long, Goldilocks
was fast asleep.

Soon the three bears
came back from their
walk in the woods.

"Someone's been eating my porridge!"

said Papa Bear.

"Someone's been eating my porridge!"
said Mama Bear.

"Someone's been eating my porridge!"
said Baby Bear.
"And it's all gone!"

"Someone's been sitting in my chair!"

said Papa Bear.

"Someone's been sitting in my chair!" said Mama Bear.

"Someone's been sitting in my chair!" said Baby Bear. **"And it's broken!"**

Then the three bears walked into the bedroom.

"Someone's been sleeping in my bed!"

said Papa Bear.

"Someone's been sleeping in my bed!"

said Mama Bear.

"Someone's
been sleeping
in my bed!"

said Baby Bear.

"And look!
She's still there!"

22

Just then Goldilocks woke up.
She saw the three bears.
They looked **VERY** angry.

Goldilocks jumped out of bed.
She ran right out of the house.

And she ran and she ran
as fast as she could,
all the way home.